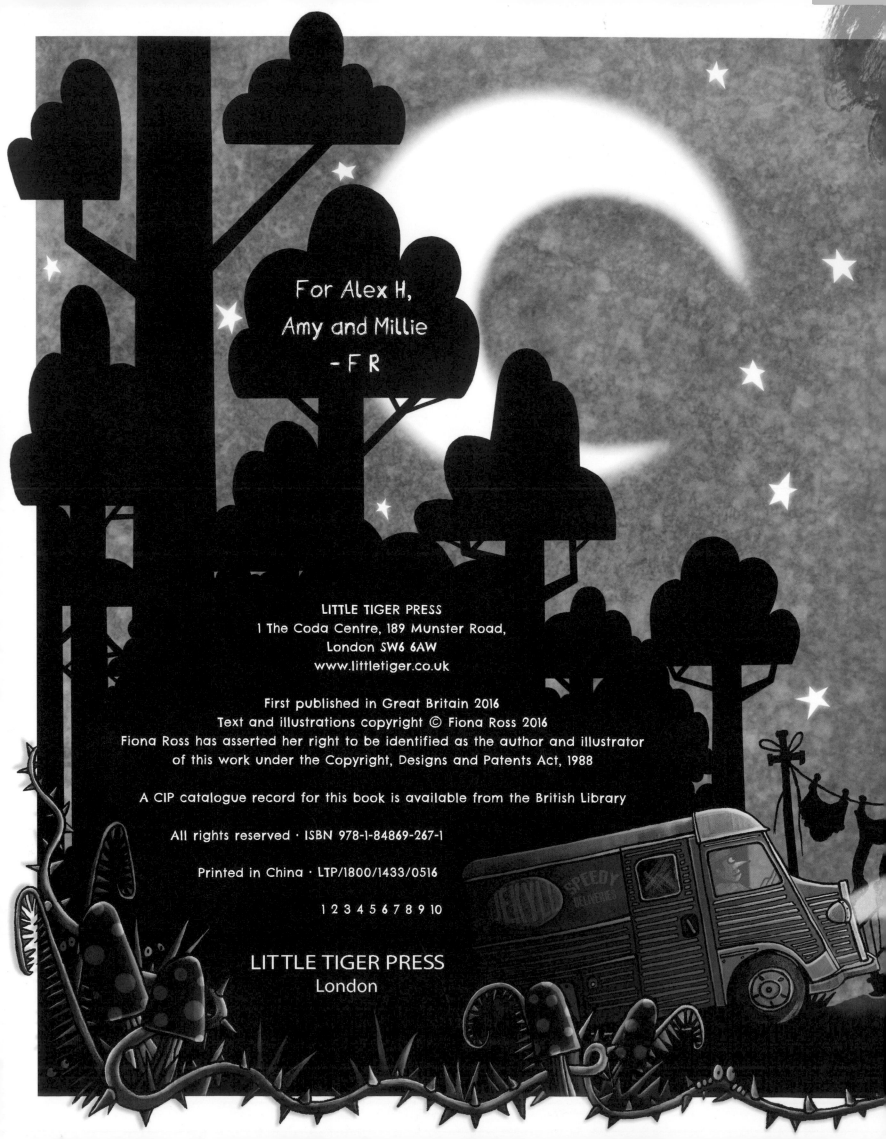

For Alex H,
Amy and Millie
- F R

LITTLE TIGER PRESS
1 The Coda Centre, 189 Munster Road,
London SW6 6AW
www.littletiger.co.uk

First published in Great Britain 2016
Text and illustrations copyright © Fiona Ross 2016
Fiona Ross has asserted her right to be identified as the author and illustrator
of this work under the Copyright, Designs and Patents Act, 1988

Printed in China · LTP/1800/1433/0516

1 2 3 4 5 6 7 8 9 10

LITTLE TIGER PRESS
London

Hyde
and
Squeak

FIONA ROSS

Late at night,
if you hear a knock at
the door, it's best not to answer.
YOU wouldn't, would you? Because you
may just find a mysterious . . .

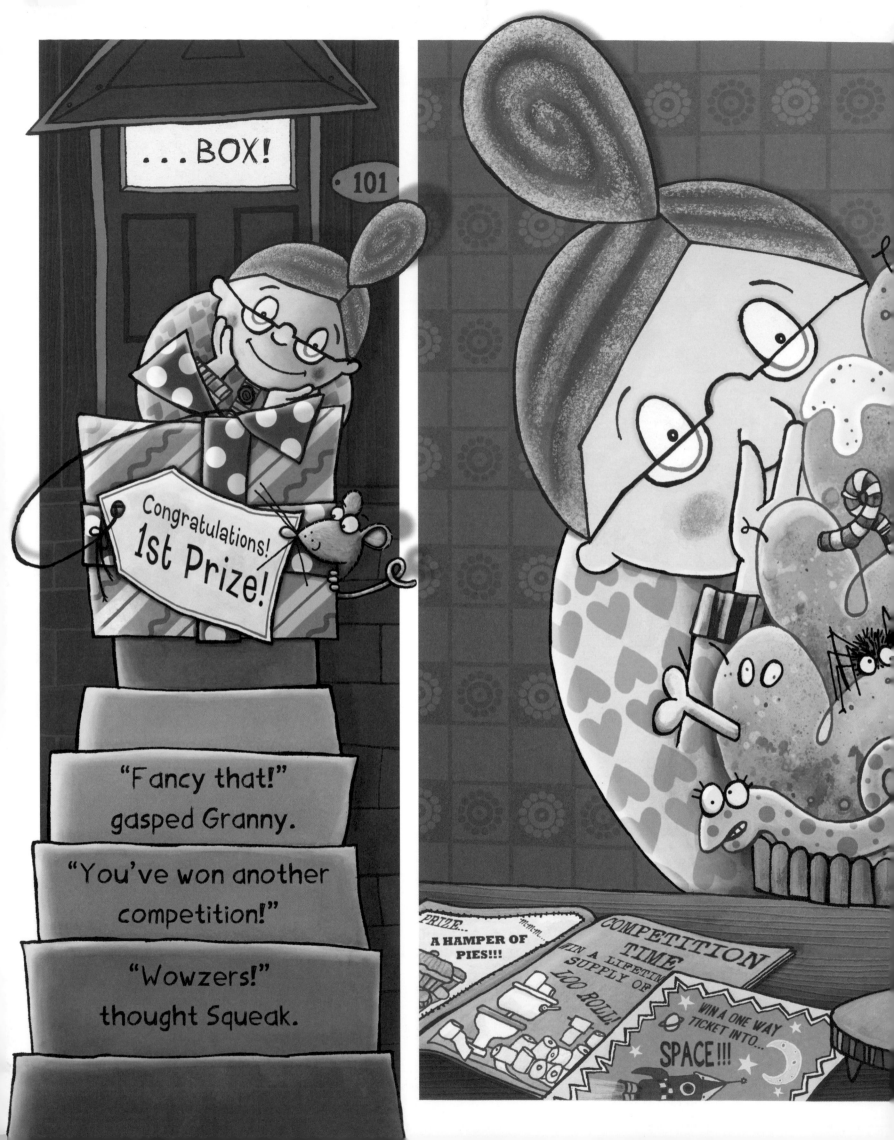

. . . BOX!

101

Congratulations!
1st Prize!

"Fancy that!"
gasped Granny.

"You've won another
competition!"

"Wowzers!"
thought Squeak.

PRIZE... mmm...
A HAMPER OF
PIES!!!

COMPETITION
TIME
WIN A LIFETIME
SUPPLY OF
LOO ROLL!

WIN A ONE WAY
TICKET INTO...
SPACE!!!

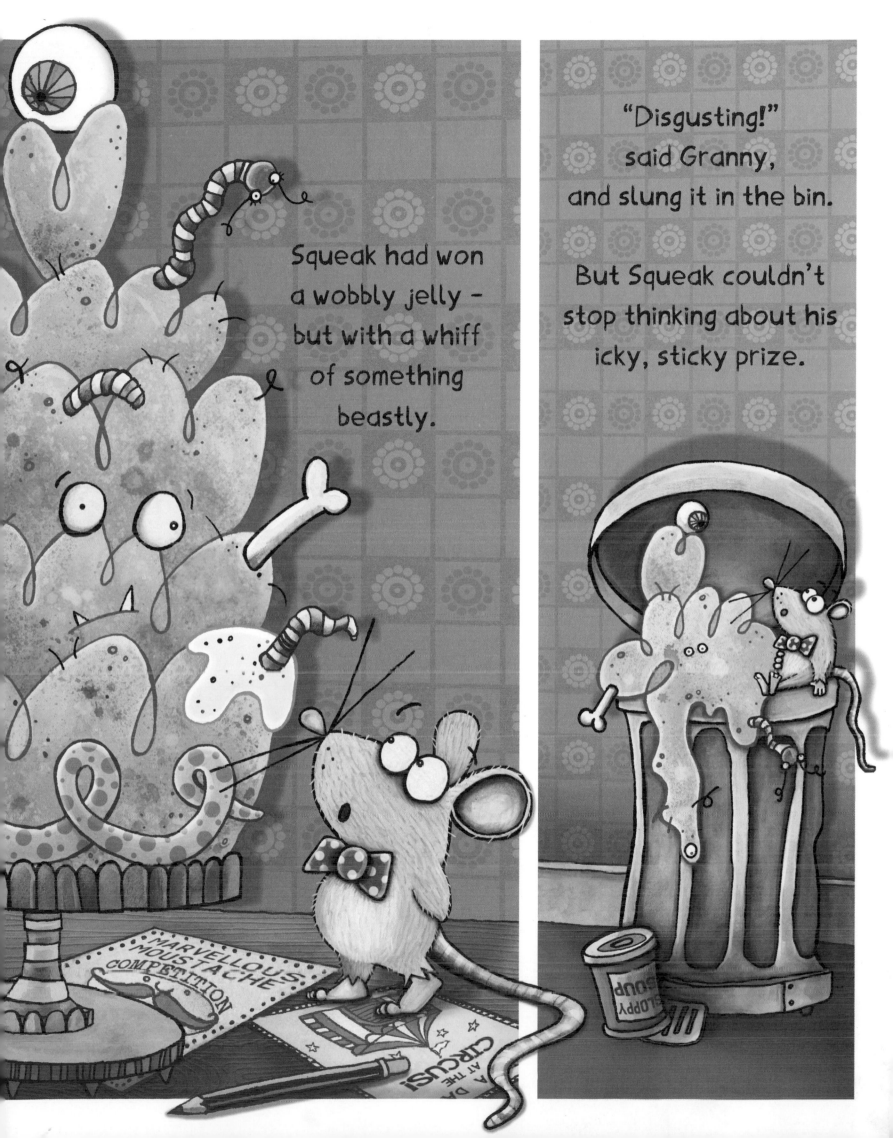

Squeak had won a wobbly jelly – but with a whiff of something beastly.

"Disgusting!" said Granny, and slung it in the bin.

But Squeak couldn't stop thinking about his icky, sticky prize.

MARVELLOUS MOUSTACHE COMPETITION

Squeak grunted and growled.

He burped and slurped . . .

That night, when Granny was softly snoring, Squeak tiptoed downstairs. "I'll just have a taste," he thought. What a bad idea!

YUCK!

First he gobbled the food in the cupboards.

Then he guzzled the snacks in the fridge.

Every last one!

"I NEED MORE GRUB!" roared Hyde, and he telephoned for a super-sized supper.

Poor Granny woke to a TERRIBLE MESS!

"We've been robbed!" she cried.

She tidied up, then set off to buy breakfast.

Soon after, there was a knock at the door. And guess what?

But Hyde was on a mission.

BANG!

CRASH!

FIZZ! FLASH!

In no time at all . . .

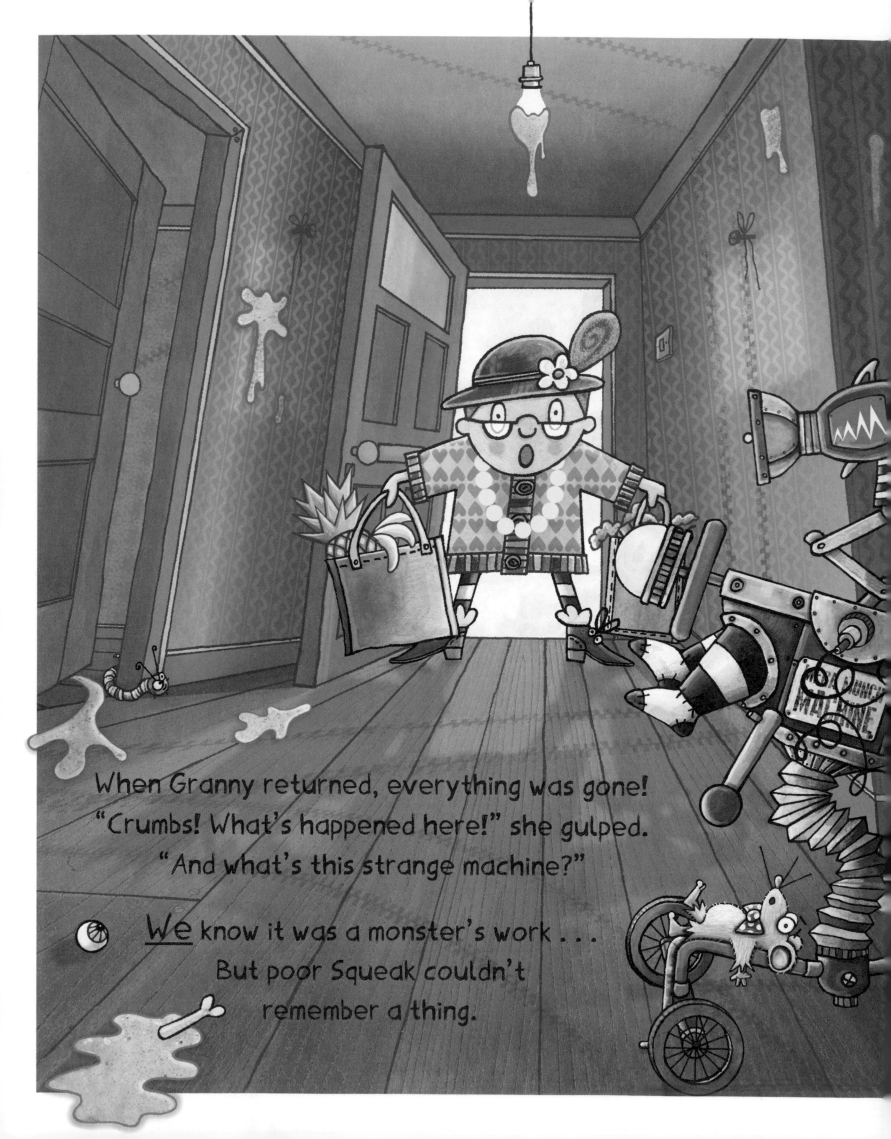

When Granny returned, everything was gone!
"Crumbs! What's happened here!" she gulped.
"And what's this strange machine?"

<u>We</u> know it was a monster's work . . .
But poor Squeak couldn't
remember a thing.

So Granny telephoned the police. "We'd like to report a robbery," she said.

"It's been happening all over town," said the policeman. "Luckily, we have a photo of the crook . . ."

"Don't worry, Squeak," said Granny. "I won't let anything happen to you!"

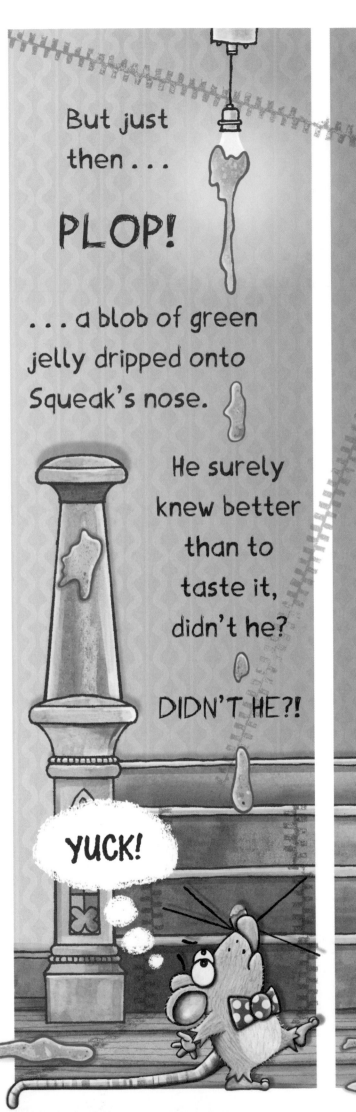

But just then . . .

PLOP!

. . . a blob of green jelly dripped onto Squeak's nose.

He surely knew better than to taste it, didn't he?

DIDN'T HE?!

YUCK!

Squeak grunted and growled and burped and slurped.
And he grew and grew and grew until . . .

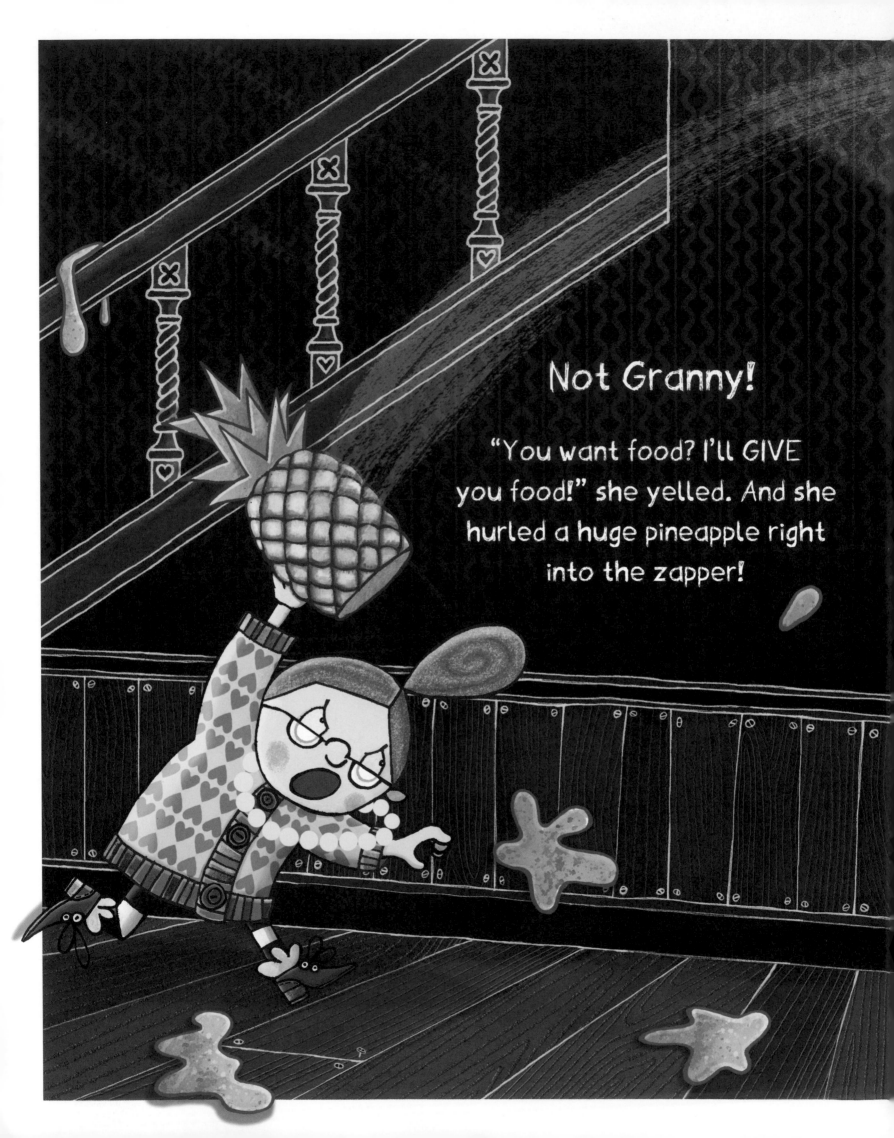

Not Granny!

"You want food? I'll GIVE you food!" she yelled. And she hurled a huge pineapple right into the zapper!

"My dear,
dear Squeak!"
cried Granny, and
she jumped for joy
to see him.

Soon things
were almost
back to normal.

Phew!

"I knew that jelly was trouble!" said Granny. "Let's not win any more of those!"

Squeak nodded.

No more jellies.

But he STILL loved a competition . . .